Alma Louise
Plans a Picnic

written and illustrated by

Melissa Smith Turner

ISBN: 9781497404533
Imprint: Independently published

Created & Printed in the U.S.A.

for:
DEAN McCOY
MILLIE GRACE
STELLA BELLE
HAL SMITH
TALLULAH HOPE

Alma Louise could run like the wind. She worked hard picking flowers to share with her friends.

The hot sunny sun made flower-picking hard work.

Alma Louise took a break and called her friend, Herk.

Herk ran to play with Alma Louise.

They talked about gardens and how to climb trees.

"A real picnic needs tomatoes, **freshly grown.**"

"I disagree," said Herk with a groan. "The best food for a picnic is ice cream on a cone."

Then, Alma Louise had a thought in her mind.

She said to her friend, "we can have more than one picnic food."

This helped Alma Louise and Herk find a better mood.

So, with
tomatoes
freshly
grown
and
ice cream
on a cone,

Alma Louise learned the best part of picnicking . . .

is not
eating
alone.

The real Alma Louise and Hursel "Herk" (pictured above on a Sunday afternoon in 1989) were married for over six decades. Their love survived many debates over tomatoes and ice cream and other important things. *MeeMaw and PeePaw* are a true picture of hard work, loyalty, and commitment.

ABOUT THE AUTHOR

Melissa Smith Turner (granddaughter of Alma Louise and Hursel) enjoys doodling silly rhyming stories for her husband and five children. She discovered her love of doodling while taking notes in fifth grade history class. She perfected her sketches during High School science and College literature classes. Today, she creatively illustrates church notes, grocery lists, and little stories like Alma Louise.

Made in the USA
Middletown, DE
15 May 2023

30630151R00018